Dedicated to:
Faith Angelina Dixon

Invasion of the Grumpies

Written by Thal Dixon
Illustrated by Jim Hawks

In the moonlight they're descending
Like the shadows from the trees,
Seeking unsuspecting families
Like a swarm of angry bees.

They are mean and nasty Grumpies.
They're a family's greatest vice.
They want all the world unhappy.
They hate everything that's nice.

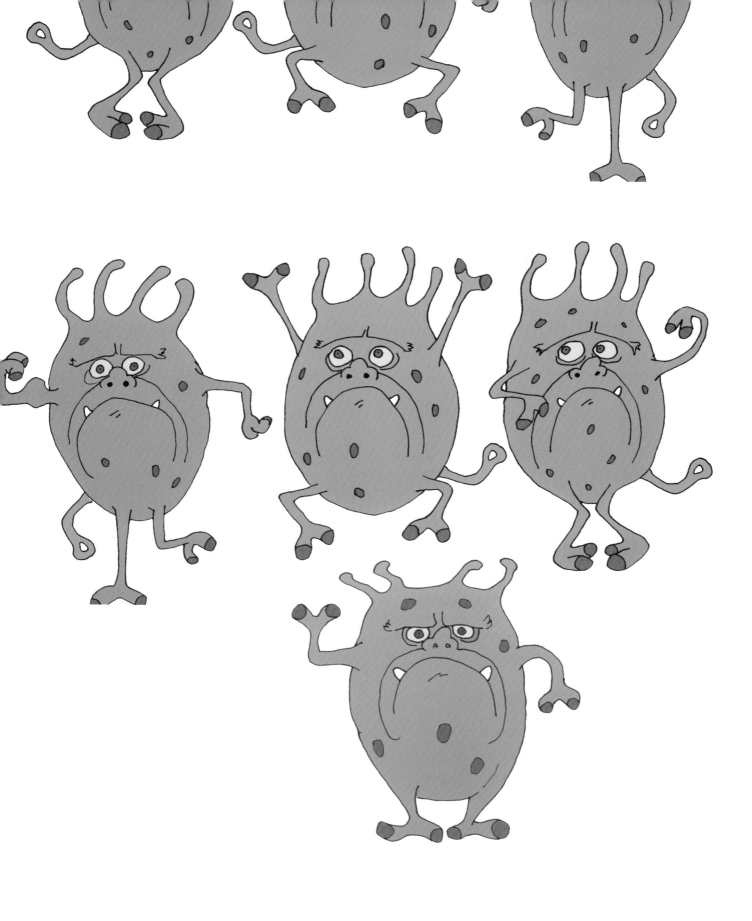

Every night the Grumpies gather
On the rooftops of each town,
Listening in through all the chimneys
Picking which ones to go down.

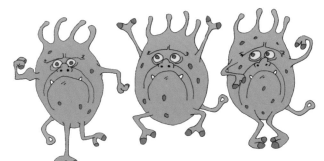

Will our families all surrender?
Will the Grumpies take control?
Everyday more people struggle
While the Grumpies take their toll.

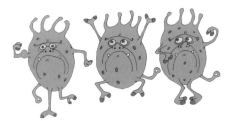

As the sun shines through the mountains
Turning nighttime into day,
Grumpies slide down certain chimneys
Their invasion underway.

Running quickly through the silence
They team up and work in pairs.
They go flying through the kitchen,
Down the hallways, up the stairs.

Grumpies search in every bedroom
For the people as they sleep,
Like small groups of trained commandos
Passing signals as they creep.

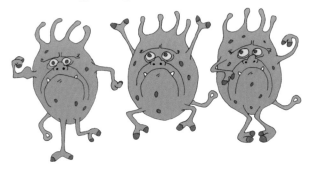

Getting set in their positions
As the households slowly wake,
They unleash their deadly poisons
Just to see which families break.

"I don't want to!" shouted Sister,
As she stomped her foot some more.
"You'll be sorry," Mother answered,
"If I have to count to four."

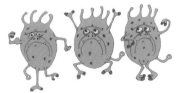

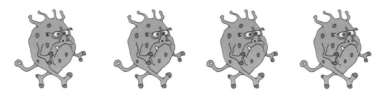

"You can't make me!" argued Brother,
"I don't care and I won't go!"
"School is boring and I hate it!"
"Every day I tell you so!"

One by one each nasty comment
Seemed to float into the air,
While the grumpies remained hidden,
Two inside of Sister's hair.

As each family stood there fighting,
All the hiding grumpies cheered.
Then at last the spell was broken
By the words all grumpies feared.

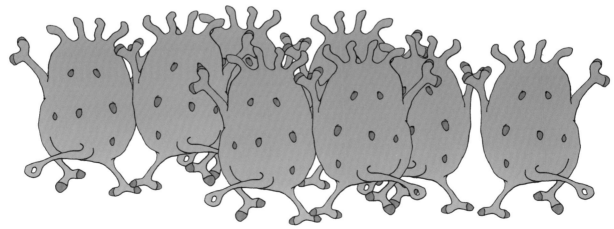

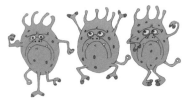

"I am sorry," said one mother,
As she hugged her daughter tight.
"Did you wake up kind of grumpy?
I know how to make things right."

Mother gently gave her kisses.
Then she sent her out to play.
And that little girl once frowning,
Was sent smiling on her way.

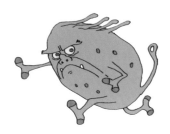

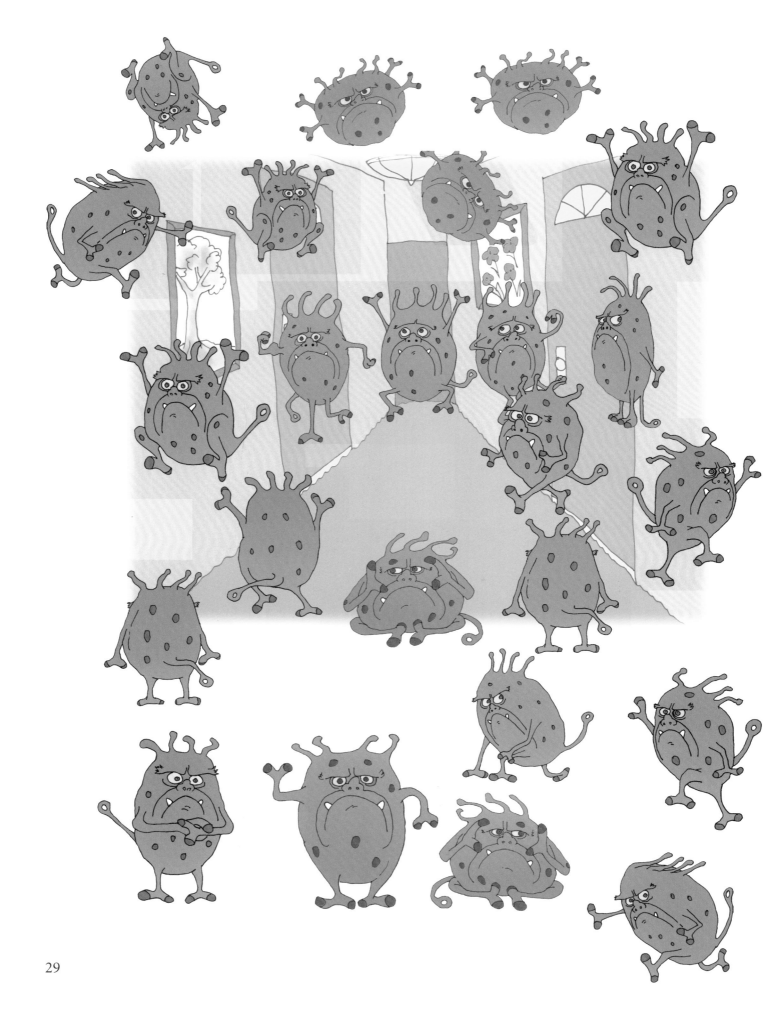

Grumpies groaned and growled in anger
Not believing what they heard.
All their plans were being ruined.
Would more mothers get the word?

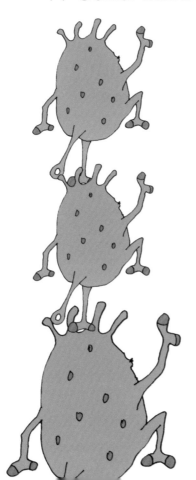

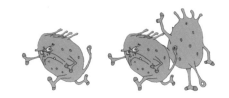

What if all their grumpy tactics
Failed to change this special Mom?
Would her kindness be contagious?
Was it love that kept her calm?

In an act to save resources,
Or avoid a sure defeat,
Many grumpies jumped from hiding
And took off in full retreat.

They went flying through the hallways
To the chimneys they came down.

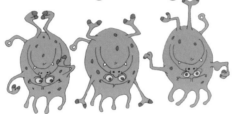

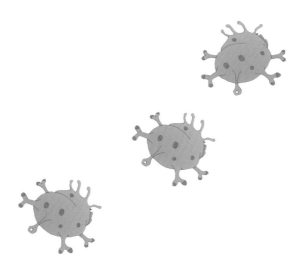

Then went over all the roof tops
As they hurried out of town.

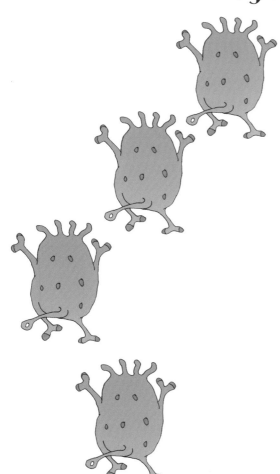

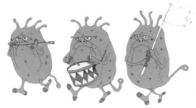

Though they left behind some stragglers
That on some days try to fight,
It's the simple phrase "I love you,"
That can always make things right.

So just say it every morning
And again each end of day.
Say "I love you," when you mean it,
And the grumpies go away.

The End

Inspiration for Invasion of the Grumpies

Like many great stories, Invasion of the Grumpies, was inspired by real life. The main idea came from an experience I had with my five year old daughter, Faith. I came down on a Saturday morning for breakfast and Faith was complaining about something to her mother. She had her arms folded, her head down, and she had a big frown on her face. As I walked by and read the "please help me here," look on the face of my wife, Claudia, I tossed Faith's hair around and asked her questioningly, "What's the matter? Do you have Grumpies in your hair or something?" Right then I knew I had an idea for another story. One week later, Invasion of the Grumpies was written.

Let's face it, all of us are grumpy at times and our loved ones are usually the ones dealing with it. When we attack the person for being grumpy then the situation usually gets worse. However, when we respond in kindness then we usually get a more positive result and the grumpiness goes away faster. Invasion of the Grumpies helps kids and adults to address the behavior and not the person. This is a lesson that we all need to be reminded of often…

Dedicated to:

Faith Angelina Dixon

For more on the Grumpies please visit one of our sites below

Visit our web site : www.GrumpyPublications.com

Visit our Facebook Page: Invasion of the Grumpies

Thal Dixon-Poet Author

I have always enjoyed writing since my earliest days in school. I love giving life to new ideas, characters and adventures. I first discovered my gift for rhyming poetry when a poet came to visit my English class in the 8th grade. I have been writing my own poetry and stories ever since. As a father of five, I have always enjoyed reading and sharing stories and adventures with my own children. I now look forward to sharing them with yours.

Jim Hawks-Illustrator

I have been an artist all my life. My passion is to create and I have been blessed with many talents. I am a former art director and now have my own company Hawkart Design Services. This book is a collaboration with a friend and we hope you enjoy it. I enjoy philosophy, ancient cultures and histories, metaphysics, human evolution, Neuro Linguistic Programming, yoga, meditation and inspirational stories and books. My websites: jimhawks.com and hawkart.us and matofindstruenorth.info

Coming Soon!

Thal Dixon-Author   **Jim Hawks-Illustrator**

A book that explores the selfish motives of a bully and how those
selfish desires will always lead to an unhappy ending.

See what's new at www.GrumpyPublications.com

Now Available!

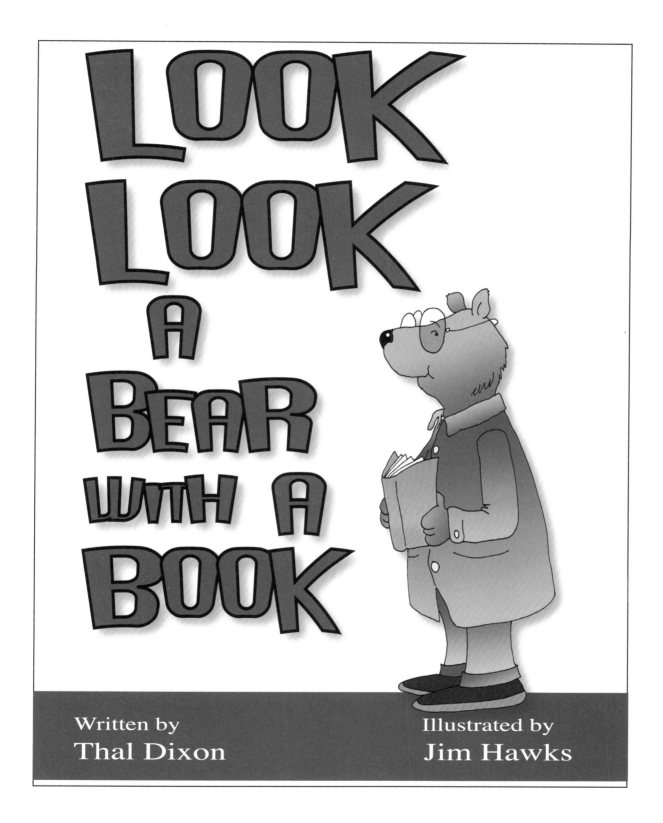

LOOK LOOK A BEAR WITH A BOOK

Written by
Thal Dixon

Illustrated by
Jim Hawks

A delightful book about two bored kids that meet up with a talking bear that takes them on all kinds of adventures with his magical book. The bear teaches them that reading can take you anywhere you want to go.